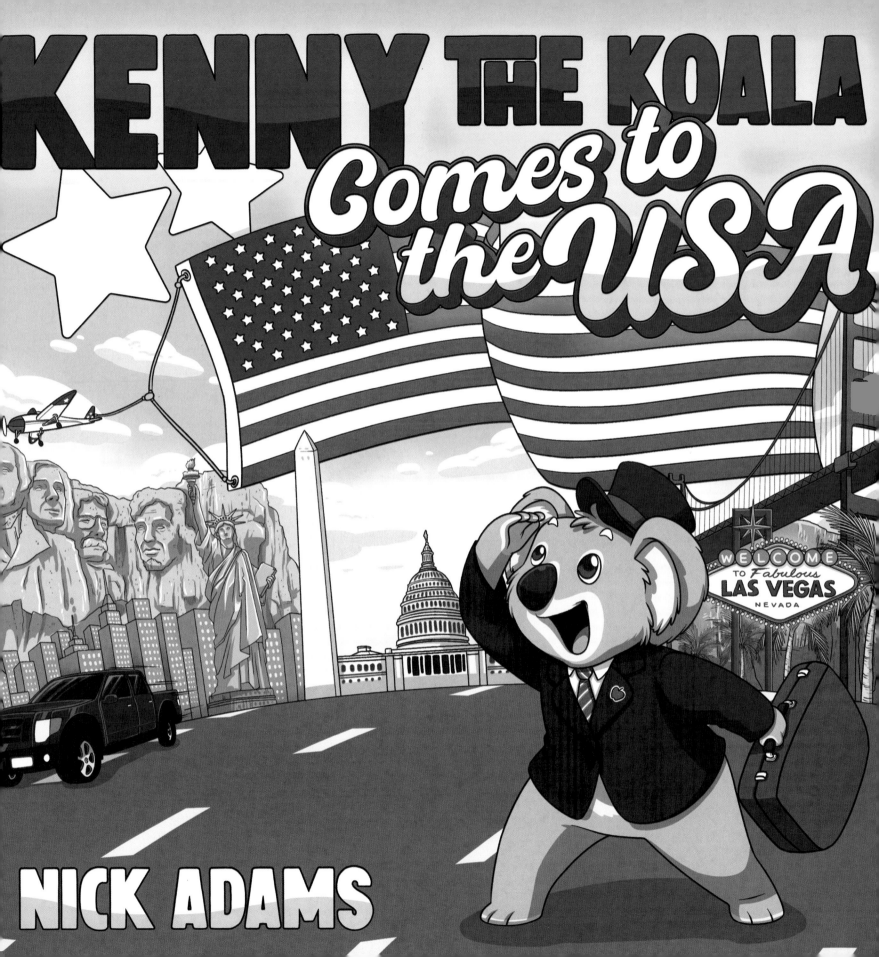

A POST HILL PRESS BOOK
ISBN: 978-1-63758-907-6

Cover Design by Cody Corcoran
Interior Design and Typography by Alana Mills

Post Hill Press
New York • Nashville
posthillpress.com

Published in the United States of America

1 2 3 4 5 6 7 8 9 10

To my mom and dad—the people that made my dream possible

KENNY THE KOALA
Comes to the USA

NICK ADAMS

One night in Australia, a sleepy koala named Kenny sat on the floor watching TV.

He was about to go to bed when something new came on!

It was an American show! Kenny was instantly mesmerized.

The United States seemed so big! Everyone talked differently than he did. Everything seemed big and exciting.

There were people from all over the world there, and they all had different jobs and different goals.

It sounded like a place where anyone could follow their dreams—in fact, Kenny heard someone on the TV call it the *American Dream.*

DID YOU KNOW?

The United States has been called the *Melting Pot* because of its diverse population. In fact, there are more than 350 different languages spoken across the country!

Right then, Kenny decided that was exactly what he wanted. He was going to go to the USA!

Kenny wanted to see all of the things he'd heard about, so he made a bucket list.

The very next day, he
packed his bags and
kissed his parents
goodbye.

"Be safe!" his mom said.
"Take lots of pictures!"

The plane ride was very long—almost an entire day!

Kenny made sure to bring lots of things to pass the time.

DID YOU KNOW?

On a straight-line path, Australia is about 9,463 miles from the United States. That's over nineteen hours of flight time!

When the plane landed, Kenny was so excited to start exploring. Right away, he could tell the United States was different from home!

He got to drive on massive roads called interstates that connected all the states together.

He tried lots of yummy American food, like juicy hamburgers and sticky barbecue and crispy fried chicken.

He even went to a football game.

He was so excited to watch the cheerleaders perform!

Kenny made sure to take lots of pictures of the places he visited like his parents asked.

In New York, he got to climb inside the Statue of Liberty.

DID YOU KNOW?

The Statue of Liberty was a birthday gift from France to the United States! It took twenty-one years to build and was given to the United States in 1884. There are 354 steps between the ground and the crown.

In Washington D.C., he got to see the White House.

He couldn't wait to show his parents that he'd been where the President lives!

In Florida, he got some sun at the beach, went to Disney World...

...and even visited a little town that looked just like Greece!

DID YOU KNOW?

Tarpon Springs, Florida, has a higher population of Greek Americans than anywhere else in the US. From street names in Greek to Greek restaurants and architecture, Tarpon Springs is a little slice of Greece in America!

He listened to country music in Tennessee, went to a rodeo in Texas, and went to Hollywood in California.

Before long, he had checked everything off his bucket list!

Kenny loved the United States with all of its sights and sounds and history. He had made so many new friends and done so many cool things.

His trip was almost over, and he was so sad. He never wanted to leave!

He knew it would be scary to make a home in a new place,
but he knew he would miss it more than anything...

So Kenny decided to stay!

To stay in the USA permanently, Kenny had to pass a test to become an American citizen.

He studied very hard, and he passed!

He was so proud to tell his parents that he was officially an American citizen.

DID YOU KNOW?

The process of becoming a U.S. citizen is called *naturalization*.

He searched and searched for the perfect place to live. Although he loved all the things he'd learned about America, he still missed home very much.

It wasn't long before Kenny found a town that reminded him of Australia! It was full of people just like him—people who loved the United States but wanted to be reminded of home.

Kenny made lots of new friends. It felt like he'd found a family!

Kenny was proud of himself for trying new things and being brave.

He realized he could inspire other people to be brave, too, so he started writing down all of the things he'd seen and done on his American adventure.

Before long, he'd written an entire book!

MY
AMERICAN
ADVENTURE

by
KENNY
THE
KOALA

Everyone loved it—even the President! He called Kenny and invited him to the White House.

Kenny got to see the President's private bowling alley and Air Force One. He made sure to get a picture to send home.

Kenny wanted to share his love of the United States with kids across the country.

He wanted to teach them to be good citizens and to take care of their country.

Encouraging them to be patriotic made him so excited!

He was invited all over the United States to talk about his experiences.

He saw a new city almost every day—deserts and oceans, mountains and canyons, places that were green and places that were covered in snow.

There was so much to see!

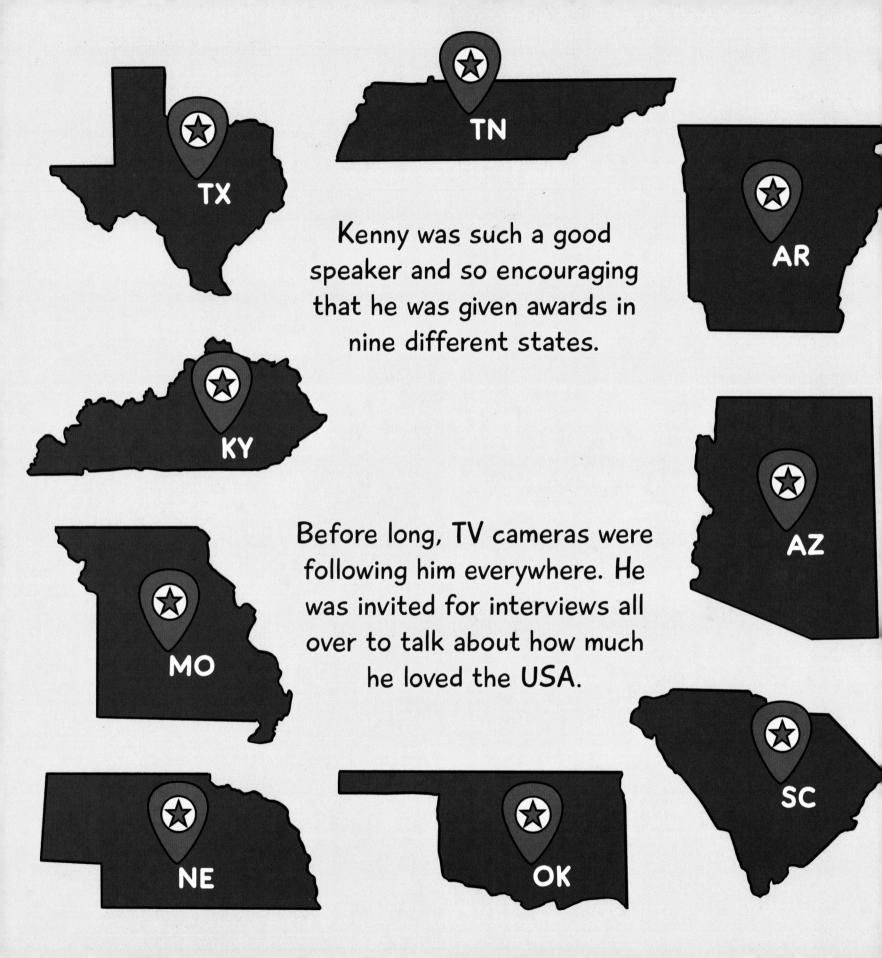

Kenny was such a good speaker and so encouraging that he was given awards in nine different states.

Before long, TV cameras were following him everywhere. He was invited for interviews all over to talk about how much he loved the USA.

He wrote many letters home to his parents, and he was always excited to get letters back from them. They missed him, but they were proud of him for being brave. His bravery had taken him on a great adventure.

And after hearing so many great things about Kenny's new home, they decided to move to the United States, too—

right down the street from Kenny!

Kenny looked around at all that he had done and all of the friends he had made.

He had chased his own American Dream and helped other people to do the same.

Tired from all of his traveling, Kenny settled down in his cozy new American home for a good night's sleep.

Tomorrow, he would do it all over again!

AUTHOR'S NOTE

Never stop dreaming. Never stop believing.

America is a very special country.
I love it, and so should you.

We are all very lucky to live here. There
is no place I would rather live.

I still get excited every day about
being in the United States.

I have been lucky to live out all of my dreams.
I could not have done this anywhere else.

I know that if you work hard, you will have
the same experience as I have had.

Always be proud to be an American.

ABOUT THE AUTHOR

Nick Adams is a motivational speaker, presidential appointee, and television commentator.

The bestselling author runs the Foundation for Liberty and American Greatness (FLAG), an organization that teaches civics and history, and helps inspire students on the power of the American Dream. More than 1.5 million K–12 students across the United States use FLAG's resources: *Student's Constitution*, *Student's Declaration of Independence*, and *Student's Federalist Papers*. For more information, please visit www.flagusa.org.

Adams contributes to numerous media organizations and has received multiple state awards, including honorary citizenship in nine states. He is a proud naturalized American citizen.

ABOUT FLAG

FLAG is the Foundation for Liberty and American Greatness, a 501(c)(3) registered educational charity aimed at promoting the American Dream and teaching civics to K-12 students.

In doing so, FLAG creates and distributes resources for students, parents, and teachers, for both in-classroom instruction as well as at home.

For more information, visit www.flagusa.org.